# Dear Parent:
# Your child's love of reading starts here!

Every child learns to read in a different way and at his or her own speed. You can help your young reader improve and become more confident by encouraging his or her own interests and abilities. You can also guide your child's spiritual development by reading stories with biblical values and Bible stories, like I Can Read! books published by Zonderkidz. From books your child reads with you to the first books he or she reads alone, there are I Can Read! books for every stage of reading:

**SHARED READING**
Basic language, word repetition, and whimsical illustrations, ideal for sharing with your emergent reader.

**1 BEGINNING READING**
Short sentences, familiar words, and simple concepts for children eager to read on their own.

**2 READING WITH HELP**
Engaging stories, longer sentences, and language play for developing readers.

**3 READING ALONE**
Complex plots, challenging vocabulary, and high-interest topics for the independent reader.

**4 ADVANCED READING**
Short paragraphs, chapters, and exciting themes for the perfect bridge to chapter books.

I Can Read! books have introduced children to the joy of reading since 1957. Featuring award-winning authors and illustrators and a fabulous cast of beloved characters, I Can Read! books set the standard for beginning readers.

A lifetime of discovery begins with the magical words *"I Can Read!"*

*Visit www.icanread.com for information on enriching your child's reading experience.*
*Visit www.zonderkidz.com for more Zonderkidz I Can Read! titles.*

"Forgive us our sins, as we also forgive everyone who sins against us. Keep us from falling into sin when we are tempted."
Luke 11:4

ZONDERKIDZ

*LarryBoy and the Mudslingers*
©2012 Big Idea Entertainment, LLC. VEGGIETALES®, character names, likenesses and other indicia are trademarks of and copyrighted by Big Idea Entertainment, LLC. All rights reserved.
Illustrations ©2011 by Big Idea Entertainment, Inc.

Requests for information should be addressed to:
Zonderkidz, 5300 *Patterson SE, Grand Rapids, Michigan 49530*

ISBN 978-0-310-73214-3

All Scripture quotations unless otherwise noted are taken from the Holy Bible, *New International Reader's Version®, NIrV®.* Copyright © 1995, 1996, 1998 by Biblica, Inc.™ Used by permission of Zondervan. All rights reserved worldwide.

Any Internet addresses (websites, blogs, etc.) and telephone numbers in this book are offered as a resource. They are not intended in any way to be or imply an endorsement by Zondervan, nor does Zondervan vouch for the content of these sites and numbers for the life of this book.

Editor: Mary Hassinger
Art direction: Karen Poth
Cover design: Karen Poth
Interior design: Ron Eddy

Printed in China

12 13 14 15 16 17 /DSC/ 6 5 4 3 2 1

 I Can Read!™ BEGINNING 1 READING

# LarryBoy and the Mudslingers

story by Karen Poth

Somewhere near Bumblyburg,

the Bad Apple made a terrible plan.

"We'll get those Veggies," she said.

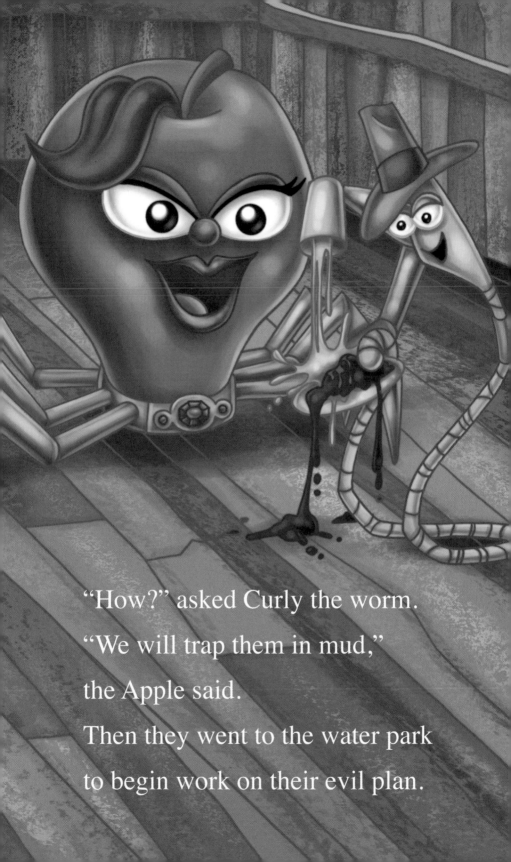

"How?" asked Curly the worm.
"We will trap them in mud,"
the Apple said.
Then they went to the water park
to begin work on their evil plan.

It was a hot day.

Junior and Laura were in the car.

They were going to the water park

just like Curly and Bad Apple.

The trip was SO long.

"Are we almost there?" Laura asked.

"We will be there soon,"

Junior's dad said.

They finally got there.

Junior and Laura lay on the beach.

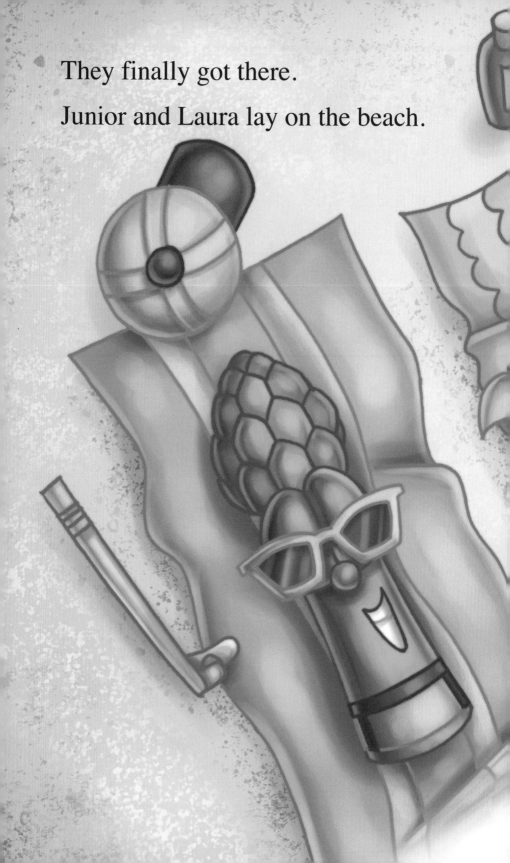

They did not see Curly.

He was in the sand.

He had a balloon filled with MUD!

When Laura closed her eyes,
Curly tossed the balloon.

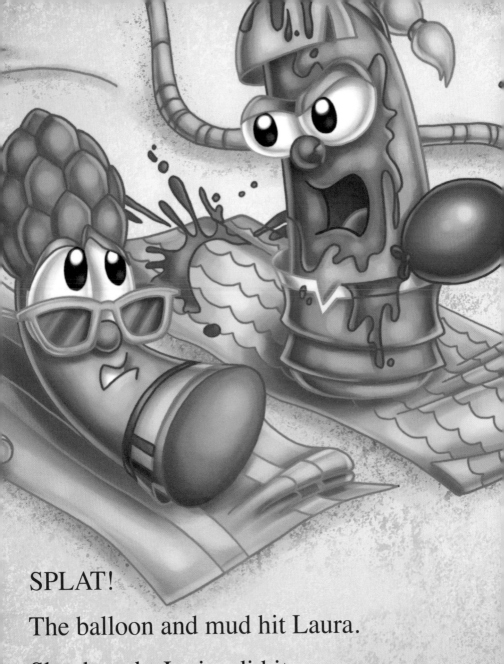

SPLAT!

The balloon and mud hit Laura.

She thought Junior did it.

"I didn't!" Junior said.

Laura didn't listen.

She threw a balloon at Junior.

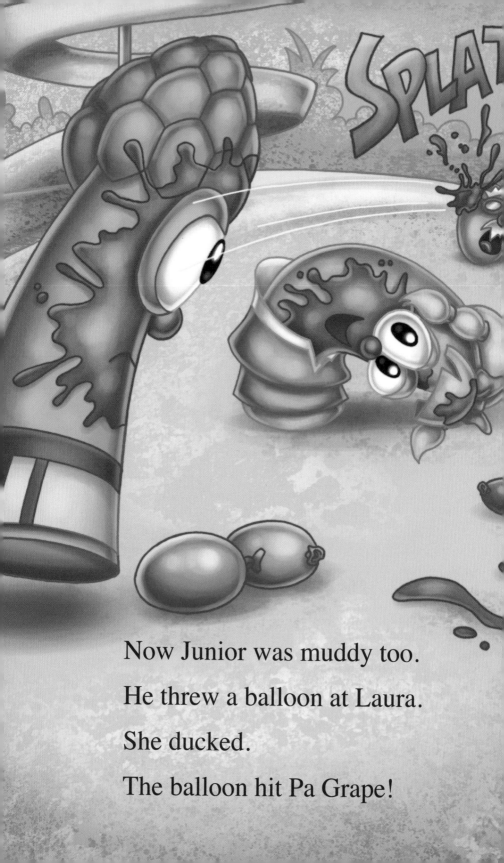

Now Junior was muddy too.

He threw a balloon at Laura.

She ducked.

The balloon hit Pa Grape!

Pa Grape got mad.

He threw a balloon at Junior.

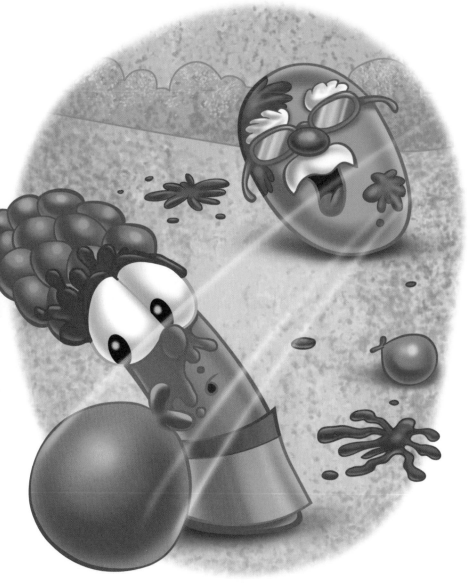

The balloon missed Junior.

It hit Jimmy Gourd!

Now Jimmy was mad too.

They needed LarryBoy.

But where was he?

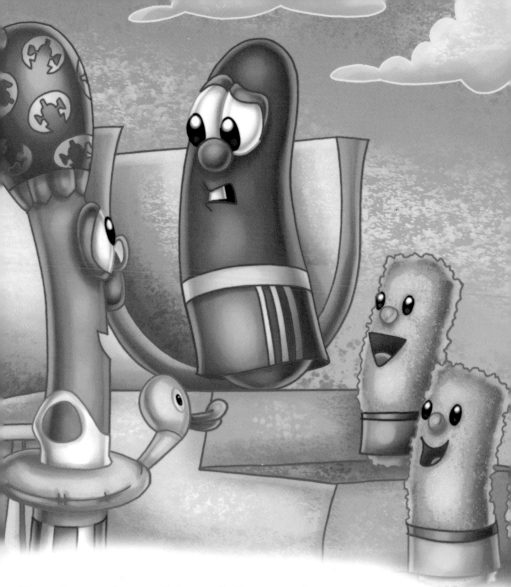

On the other side of the park,

Larry stood at the top of the slide.

He was scared!

"It will be okay, Master Larry," said Alfred.

Larry looked down.

He saw all his friends!

They were all mad.

They were all muddy!

This was a job for LarryBoy!

Larry ran to the changing room …

EVERYONE was throwing mud.
The Tater Tots, Bob the Tomato,
even Princess Petunia!
LarryBoy jumped in the middle.
"Stop!" he yelled.

SPLAT!

A balloon hit LarryBoy.

LarryBoy got mad too.

He threw a mud balloon.

It hit Alfred.

Alfred ran to the LarryMobile.

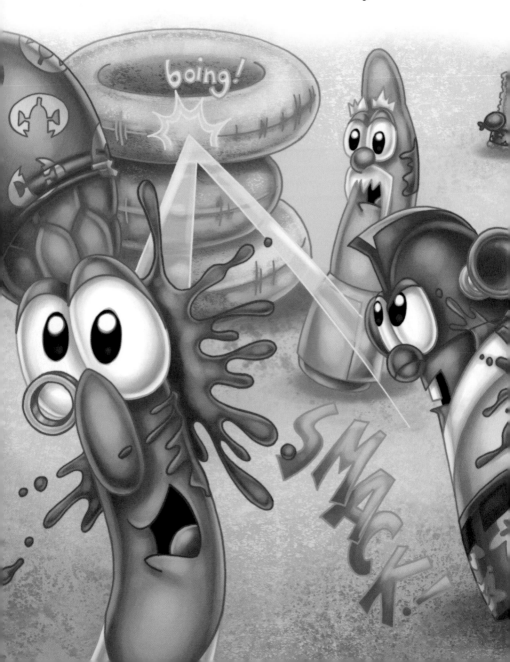

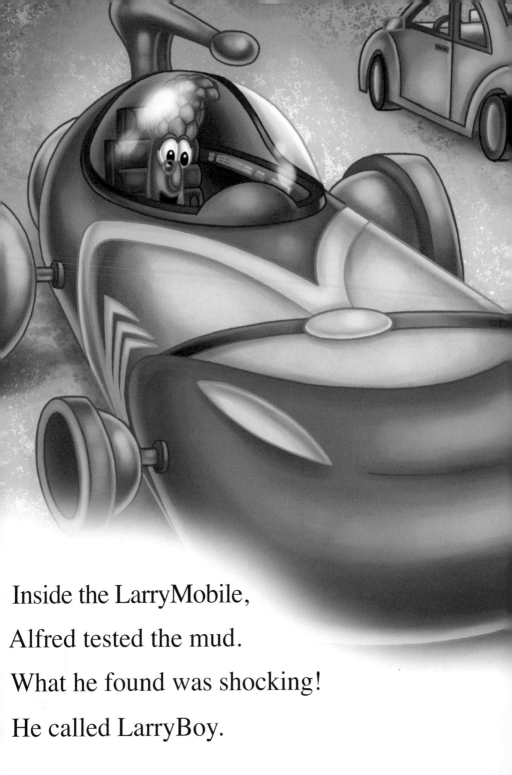

Inside the LarryMobile,
Alfred tested the mud.
What he found was shocking!
He called LarryBoy.

RING!

LarryBoy's helmet phone rang.

"What is it?" LarryBoy said.

"Stop throwing mud!"

Alfred said. "It's a trap!"

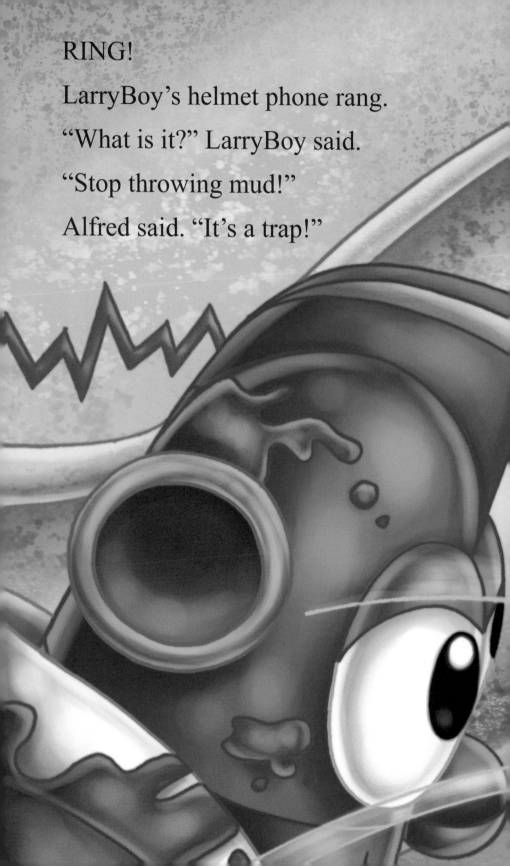

"The mud will never come off
unless you stop being mad," Alfred said.
"You must forgive each other."

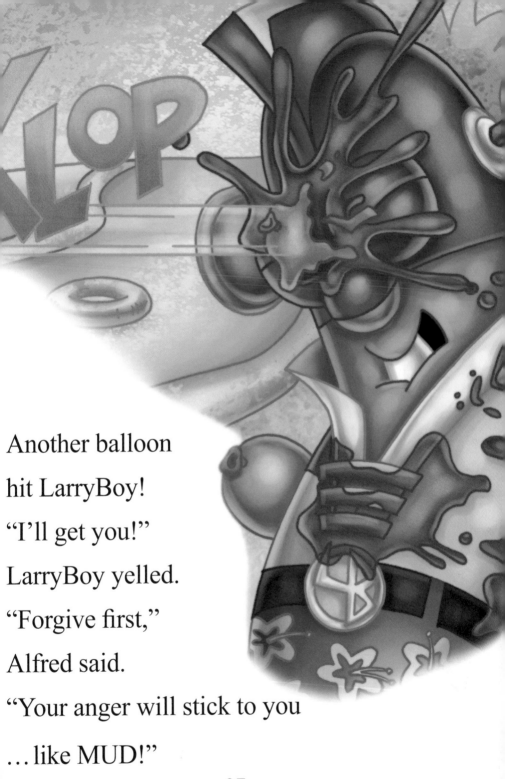

Another balloon
hit LarryBoy!
"I'll get you!"
LarryBoy yelled.
"Forgive first,"
Alfred said.
"Your anger will stick to you
…like MUD!"

The mud was trapping everyone
like flies in a spider web!

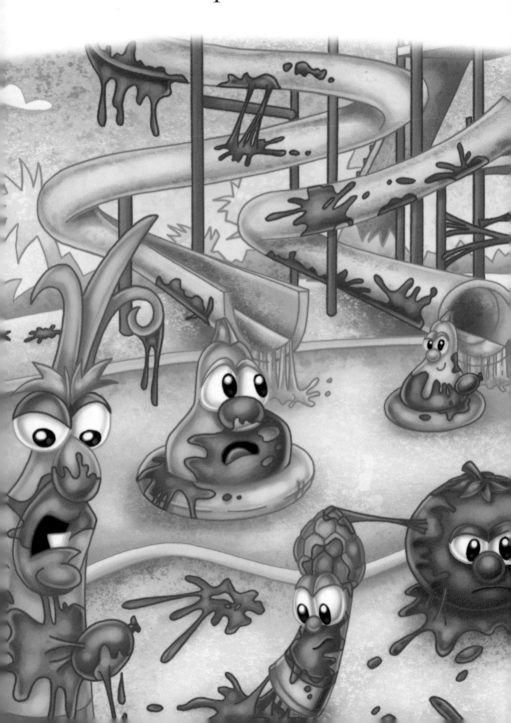

"LarryBoy," Alfred said,
"say you're sorry.
It's the only way to
stop being angry."

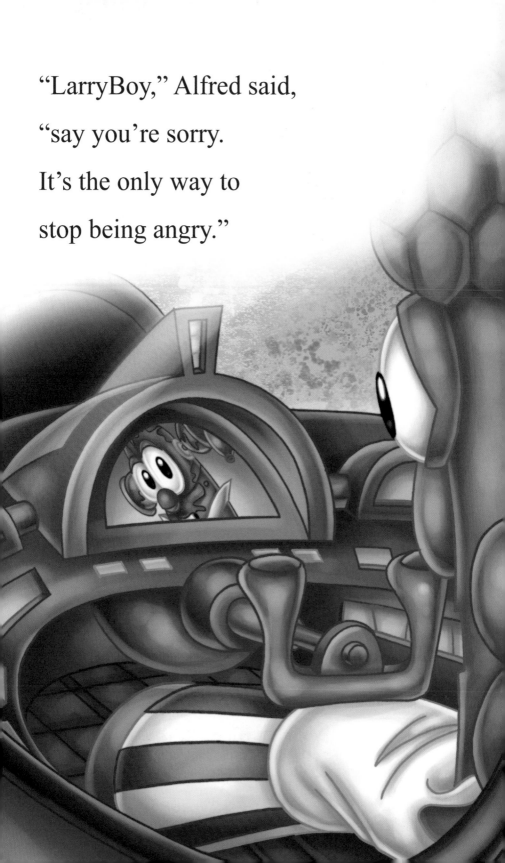

LarryBoy stopped.

"I'm sorry, Junior," he said.

Junior smiled.

"I'm sorry too," Junior said.

Soon everyone forgave each other.

The mud lost its grip.

All the Veggies played together
on the water slide.
Even LarryBoy!